Rebekkah's Journey

A WORLD WAR II REFUGEE STORY

Written by Ann E. Burg and Illustrated by Joel Iskowitz

For Norman and Sandy,
their children, their grandchildren,
and all those who came before...

ANN

—

To all who create, teach, inspire, and appreciate art.
To my mother, who encouraged my earliest efforts,
and my wife Suzanne, who inspires this artist today.

JOEL

Sleeping Bear Press

310 North Main Street, Suite 300
Chelsea, MI 48118
www.sleepingbearpress.com

THOMSON
★
GALE

© 2006 Thomson Gale, a part of the Thomson Corporation.

Thomson, Star Logo and Sleeping Bear Press are trademarks
and Gale is a registered trademark used herein under license.

Printed and bound in China.

First Edition

10 9 8 7 6 5 4 3 2 1

Library of Congress Cataloging-in-Publication Data

Burg, Ann E.
Rebekkah's journey : a WWII refugee story / written by Ann Burg ;
illustrated by Joel Iskowitz.
p. cm.
Summary: After eluding capture by the Nazis, seven-year-old Rebekkah and
her mother are brought from Italy to the United States to begin a new life.
ISBN 1-58536-275-1
1. World War, 1939-1945—Italy—Juvenile fiction. 2. World War, 1939-
1945—United States—Juvenile fiction. [1. World War, 1939-1945—Italy—
Fiction. 2. World War, 1939-1945—United States—Fiction. 3. Refugees,
Jewish—Fiction.] I. Iskowitz, Joel, ill. II. Title.
PZ7.B916258Reb 2006
[Fic]—dc22   2006002198

AUTHOR'S ACKNOWLEDGMENTS

Many people helped me to better understand the events surrounding
Rebekkah's Journey. My own journey began at the Safe Haven Museum
and Education Center in Oswego, New York. Thank you to Judy Coe
Rappaport, Lois, and all the volunteers who answered my initial ques-
tions. I am most grateful to Dr. Ruth Gruber for her moving portrait
Haven, The Unknown Story of 1,000 World War II Refugees which inspired
me to learn more about this amazing but little-known historical moment.
I am also grateful to Dr. Sharon R. Lowenstein for her book *Token Refuge,
The Story of the Jewish Refugee Shelter at Oswego, 1944-1946*, and to
the New York State Museum in Albany, for its poignant Bitter Hope
exhibit. Thanks to Ruth Fowler and Nancy Anderson of the Special
Collections Department at the Penfield Library in Oswego, and to
Alan W. Saunders, whose sister Susan was the real child who, without
being asked, gave her doll away. Most importantly, thanks to all the
former shelter residents who recorded their memories in the publication
Don't Fence Me In and the documentary *Safe Haven, A Story of Hope*. In
particular I would like to thank Rena Block, who spoke with me at
length about her experiences as a child in Oswego. My deepest gratitude
to Walter Greenberg, a former refugee, who opened his home and his
heart to my recurrent inquiries. His friendship and support has
enriched my story—and my life.

—Ann E. Burg

ILLUSTRATOR'S ACKNOWLEDGMENTS

Joel Iskowitz wishes to acknowledge the following source materials
as part of his research for his artwork.

Source photo "Refugees Arrive from Europe" (p. 14) used with
permission Alfred Eisenstaedt/Time Life Pictures/Getty Images

Source photos "Friendship Fence" (p. 14) and "Refugees in Food Line"
(p. 22) from the book *Don't Fence Me In: Memories of the Fort
Ontario Refugees and Their Friends*, published by Safe Haven Inc.

Source photo "Scene on First St." (p. 44) from Library of Congress
Prints and Photographs Division, FSA/OWI Collection, #LC USW3-
034547-D (Marjory Collins, photographer)

TO MY READERS

I first stumbled onto the story of the Fort Ontario Emergency Refugee Shelter when I was researching for another book. Although I knew that millions of Jewish people had been forced from their homes during the Holocaust, I did not know that President Franklin Roosevelt had invited 1,000 displaced individuals to stay on a vacant army base in Oswego, New York. Here they were to be given food and shelter for the remainder of World War II. In July 1944, 982 individuals from 18 different countries departed from Italy on the *Henry Gibbins,* a U.S. Army transport ship carrying wounded soldiers back to the United States.

Rebekkah's Journey is a story of this event. Every person who traveled on the *Henry Gibbins* demonstrated incredible courage during a horrific moment in world history. In choosing to create a fictional character I hoped to weave the experiences of many into a simple but authentic narrative. Although my character is fictionalized, her experiences are not.

The residents of the Fort Ontario Emergency Refugee Shelter remained behind the fence in Oswego for 18 months. Although they had signed papers to return to their homelands when the war was over, most wanted to stay in the United States and were eventually allowed to do so. First as strangers and then as American citizens, the former residents of the Fort Ontario Emergency Refugee Shelter have enriched our society in countless ways.

One last note: Some of you may wonder if Rebekkah ever sees her Papa again. I can only tell you that some families separated during the war were reunited when the war was over—but many families were not. If that saddens you—as it saddens me—perhaps it will help us to remember the importance of tolerance and the impact of kindness.

Ann E. Burg

Above us dark clouds still blocked the sun, but the rain had finally stopped. Everyone on deck was whispering excitedly. Mama gently ran her fingers through my hair.

"Maybe today, Rebekkah," she said. "Maybe today."

Even though there was little room on deck, children tagged and chased one another in small circles. Barefoot boys stood watching each other, each one waiting for the other to make a move. Two old men played chess.

Suddenly we saw her. She just appeared through the fog like an enchanted Queen of the Ocean. Some of the grown-ups started to cry.
"*Bella signora!*"
"She's so beautiful—so strong."
"Praise God!" they whispered as they waved to her.

But I saw only how big she was, how serious she looked with her green arm stretched high, holding a flaming torch. I felt afraid and hid myself in Mama's skirt.

"Now is not the time to be afraid," Mama said. "Now is the time to open our eyes and raise our voices in thanksgiving."

The rabbi moved through the crowd and the ship became quiet, waiting for him to speak.

"Baruch Ata Adonai, Eloheinu Melech ha-olam," he began. His long black beard barely moved as he spoke. "Praised are You, Eternal our God, Ruler of the universe, for granting us life, for sustaining us, and for helping us to reach this day."

As the rabbi blessed us with the words of Mama's favorite prayer, I turned my head to look at the people surrounding him.

We looked so strange! Most of us were wearing old and torn clothes. Some of the men were wearing dirty striped pajamas and shoes made out of cardboard. I hadn't any shoes at all.

My shoes had fallen off my feet when we escaped from the Nazis. First one shoe and the next day the other. For miles Mama carried me on her back. But then she grew tired. "Rebekkah," she whispered into my hair as she put me down. "Please Bekah, be strong."

I followed Mama up the mountain and did not stop even when I lost my shoe. I climbed and climbed until Mama stooped to lift me again. She stumbled, and a boy came and took me in his arms. He was so pale and white, at first I thought he was an angel. He lifted me out of Mama's arms and carried me until we stopped to rest. Then the boy angel put me down and disappeared into the darkness.

Mama found us a spot under a tree. She took one of Papa's shirts from the bundle she was carrying and wrapped it around us both.

Papa's shirt still smelled of paint from his studio and it almost felt like he was with us again. Mama held me close and rocked me like a baby even though I am almost eight. I fell asleep thinking of Papa, still running with one shoe even in my dreams.

Now there would be no more running.
We were in America. We were going to be free.

Somewhere on the ship a voice shouted words
I didn't understand. Everyone began talking in
voices and languages that were strange to me.

Mama listened carefully. "We'll stay on the
ship one more night." she said. "Tomorrow we
take a short ride on another boat, and then a
train to our new home." She took my face in her
hands. Her dark black eyes softened. "Our long
journey is almost over," she whispered.

I wished Papa were with us to celebrate.

That night Mama let me stay up later than usual. The lights from the city twinkled like stars. In Italy when we were running and hiding, everything was always black. In the convent where we hid, even the windows were painted black, and I would close my eyes tight and try to sleep so I wouldn't be afraid.

Now I wanted to stay up all night just to look at the twinkling lights, but Mama wouldn't let me. "Tomorrow will be a busy day," she said.

I thought that I should never fall asleep, but I must have, because in the morning Mama kissed me awake—and there was music and sweet bread and Mama almost happy.

American soldiers lined us up and we waited to leave the ship. With numbered tags around our necks, we waited until it was our turn to board the ferry and then, in a short while, we were on the train to our new home.

"A fence! They bring us to America to put us behind a fence!"

The rocking of the train had put me to sleep but now I awoke with fear. Again I heard a man say, "A fence! How can there be a fence in America?" Some people tried to quiet him, but others agreed. "We thought we would be free." Then the train stopped and everyone was quiet.

We had not eaten during the night and now it seemed a thousand arms were reaching through the open windows of the train, handing us small glass bottles of milk and packages of cookies.

The soldiers told us to gather our things. Some people had old suitcases tied with rope, but most of us had nothing but ourselves. Mama had just one small bundle.

I remembered the doll that Mama and Papa gave me when I was five. She was beautiful, with long lashes that opened and closed, and soft curls the color of chocolate. Her dress and coat were made of blue velvet and she had a matching hat and a soft white muff. I took her everywhere with me, even when we were hiding.

But on that last night, while I was still sleeping, someone lifted me and carried me away, forgetting my doll. I cried when I woke and wanted to go back for her but Mama said we couldn't.

"Rebekkah, you mustn't cry," she said. "The Nazis will hear you." I stopped crying out loud, but Mama knew I still cried on the inside. "My Bekah," she whispered as she rocked me. "I'm so sorry, my Bekah, I'm so sorry."

Now Mama held my hand as we climbed down the steps of the train. Everywhere people were watching us.

I was afraid, but Mama squeezed my hand three short times—*I Love You*—like she did when we were hiding. Two more short squeezes meant *Be Brave*. I held her hand tightly and we shuffled along the street and behind the fence.

There was a large grassy square. A row of white buildings was on one side. On the other side houses looked like they were built right into the hill. In the distance a big lake shimmered like a field of tiny stars.

We waited in a line until it was finally our turn
to stop at a long wooden table. A woman looked at
the tag around Mama's neck. She smiled at me and
made a mark on the papers in front of her. Then she
nodded us in the direction of another line.

There were lines for soap and lines for towels and best of all,
lines for juice and cookies! Rows and rows of juice poured into
cups made out of paper were set up on long tables. And cookies!
So many cookies! I stuffed them into my mouth and into my pockets.

"Rebekkah! Leave some for the others!" Mama said,
dragging me to another line.

This time men in uniforms asked Mama to open her bundle. Inside were two of Papa's shirts and a small silver frame with a picture of Mama and Papa on their wedding day. The glass was broken but the picture was as perfect as it was when it sat on Mama's nightstand.

Papa looked so handsome and so happy that I wanted to cry just to see him again.

A woman in a gray uniform with a red cross on her hat waved for Mama and me to follow her. She led us into a long white building. I could not believe what I saw!

More food!

Slices of bread, jars of peanut butter, bowls and bowls of marmalade and eggs! I never knew there could be so much food. The bread was white and squishy. Some of the grown-ups grumbled for heavy black bread, but I had never tasted anything so fluffy and good.

When my pockets were sagging with white bread and cookies, the woman with the red cross on her hat again waved for us to follow her. We still had our tags on and I still had no shoes, but my stomach and pockets were stuffed, and I felt different.

We climbed the stairs of another building and then stopped before a narrow wooden door.

Mama let out a little cry and pointed to the two names printed in bold black letters. Even though I had never been to school, Mama had taught me to read and to write. I smiled when I read the names. They were *our* names. My name and Mama's name!

The American woman opened the door for us and then quietly disappeared.

The room inside was almost empty but clean. There was only a small square table, two chairs, a locker, and two narrow cots. Each cot had a packet of sheets on it. There was only one small window.

The first thing Mama did was push the cots together. Then she moved the table and the two chairs into the corner. She untied her bundle and hung Papa's shirts on one of the chairs. She kissed the broken picture frame and put it in the middle of the table.

I remembered before the war how Papa used to bring us flowers. Mama would put them in a glass vase in the middle of our dining table. The diamond-shaped cuts in the glass would catch the light from the window and make tiny rainbows on our tablecloth. Sometimes I would pretend to catch them in my hand. I loved rainbows, but I would never care to see another one if only I could see my Papa again.

Mama walked over to the cots and picked up the folded white sheets. She held them close and breathed deeply. Her shoulders trembled a little bit, and she began to cry.

Mama did not cry when the Nazis took Papa away. She did not cry when we left our home or slept in the fields. She did not cry when she climbed up the mountain or down the steps of the train.

But she cried when she held the clean white sheets.

That first night, after we had eaten again, Mama and I took a walk. People were gathered on both sides of the fence. It was noisy with so many voices in different languages calling to each other.

"*Bicicletta! Bicicletta!*" the children screamed. "Look at the bicycle!"

On the other side of the fence a boy was standing on the shoulders of another boy. A tall woman with brown hair was helping him pass a bicycle over the fence! On my side of the fence a man helped another boy lower the bicycle to the ground.

On both sides of the fence people were cheering as boys took turns riding the bicycle in wild circles. I pulled Mama's hand, "May *I* take a turn, Mama?" She shook her head sternly. "No! Stay by me!"

So many things were being tossed over the fence, sweaters and socks, and even shoes. Through the open spaces, people were passing rolled magazines, candy, and ice cream on a stick.

A girl with curly yellow hair was watching me. I was ashamed that I had no shoes and that my dress was torn, but the girl smiled and held something out to me. It was a beautiful doll with golden curls and red cheeks.

That night Mama and I each slept on a cot with a pillow and clean white sheets. One of my hands held Mama's hand and the other held onto my new doll. I was so tired that I fell right asleep.

I dreamed of a long metal fence. Mama and I were on one side, and Papa was on the other. He was holding my doll with the blue velvet dress and smiling at me.

The next morning I woke up before Mama. Very quietly I slipped onto the wooden floor. I propped my new doll at the edge of the cot, put one of Papa's shirts over my dress, and tiptoed outside.

It was just beginning to get light. I looked around to make sure that no one was watching me and then crept to the fence. A few candy and ice cream wrappers littered the ground. But I wasn't interested in candy or ice cream. I quickly grabbed a small empty bottle. Then I gathered some tiny blue wildflowers that were growing along the fence.

Mama was still sleeping when I slipped back into the room. I placed my vase of flowers beside the picture of Mama and Papa. Mama would be so pleased!

But when Mama awoke, she was not pleased.

"Rebekkah," she said, her eyes dark and fiery, "you must never again leave this room without me."

Every day after that Mama made sure she was awake before me.

Mama got a job in the camp kitchen. Some of the children were going to classes to learn English, but Mama would not let me out of her sight. Instead Mama taught me what she learned.

The sky is blue.
The clouds are white.
The sun comes up in the morning.
The sun goes down at night.

While Mama sliced onions or peeled potatoes, I played with my new doll and repeated what Mama taught me. The children learned different words. Sometimes I heard them practicing so I knew these words, too.

Three blind mice.
See how they run.

I begged Mama to let me go to class with the other children, but always Mama would say, "Not today, Bekah, not today." She looked so sad that I finally stopped asking.

"The sky is blue." I told my doll. "The clouds are white. Did you ever see such a sight in your life as three blind mice?"

Sometimes I cut pictures from magazines to decorate our room. Mama brought back an old vegetable crate and a scrap of pink cloth so I could make a bed for my doll. But I surprised Mama. I draped the cloth over the crate and made her a nightstand. I even moved Papa's picture so he would be close to her.

"You are a very clever girl," Mama said. But still she did not smile.

We were never allowed to walk on the other side of the fence. People in the kitchen complained. "It is not right," they said as they threw carrots into the big metal pot. But Mama did not complain.

"We have a roof over our heads and food to eat," she'd say, but even this did not make her smile.

Finally, the Americans
allowed us to leave the camp
for a few hours every day. In
town some people walked to
stores, others just walked along the
pretty streets looking at the houses.
Sometimes Mama and I walked with
them. I tried to remember our house,
but could only remember the convent
with its windows painted black.

Once we could walk into town, everyone
hoped the children could attend a real
school. "Please, Mama, please let me go to
school!" I begged. "In America even Jewish
children go to school."

"No!" Mama said sharply but her kitchen friends
convinced her that I *should* go with the other children.
The American teachers tested me and were amazed at
all I knew even though Mama had been my only teacher.

On the first day of school, I wore my new plaid dress, clean white socks, and shiny leather shoes. Mama brushed my hair into two ponytails. She cut the bottom of one of Papa's shirts and made a ribbon for each one.

It seemed like everybody was watching us. It was just like our first day, only this time I would be walking alone on the other side of the fence.

Tears began to crowd Mama's eyes, so I squeezed her hand three short times and then two more. I followed the other children, but turned once more to look at Mama. She nodded her head and then did something I had not seen her do in a long, long time.

Mama smiled.

Ann E. Burg

Ann Burg has been writing since early childhood and had a number of articles published throughout her decade of teaching. In 2003, the publication of her first book for Sleeping Bear Press, *E is for Empire: A New York State Alphabet*, encouraged Ann to leave teaching and pursue her writing career full-time. *Rebekkah's Journey* is Ann's fifth book and her third title with Sleeping Bear Press. She and her husband live in upstate New York with two children, a tattered bear, and a rambunctious puppy named Smudges.

Joel Iskowitz

Joel Iskowitz has created hundreds of book covers, a dozen children's books, and more than 2,000 postage stamps worldwide. His artwork has appeared in many international journals including *Watercolor* and *Exhibit Builder* Magazine. Public collections include NASA, the United States Air Force, the Museum of Catholic Art and History, and the Museum of American Illustration. Awarded bronze and silver medals in international competitions, Mr. Iskowitz has also received the NOAA citation for his Space Philately. The National Endowment for the Arts designated Mr. Iskowitz a Master Designer for the United States Mint, which creates our nation's coins and medals. He makes his home in Woodstock, New York.